books

Alphabet Fun

S Is for Score!

A Sports Alphabet

by Laura Purdie Salas

CAPSTONE PRESS

a capstone imprint

A is for **athlete**.

Athletes need speed, strength, and skill. They practice, practice, practice. They push their bodies to the limit.

B is for **ball**.

Players throw baseballs, kick soccer balls, and shoot basketballs. What ball game do you like to play?

C is for coach.

The coach is in charge. She leads practices and gives directions during games. She wants all players to do their best.

D is for **dribble**.
A basketball player moves down the court. He dribbles past the other team. Then he shoots a basket and scores.

E is for event.

Athletes play at sports events. Fans cheer. Whistles blow. The home team's colors fill the stadium. Will your team win the game?

F is for **first base**.

Swing, crack – it's a hit. Run to first base. Touch it before the first baseman tags you out. You're safe!

G is for **glove**.
Boxers wear padded gloves when they fight. Boxing gloves protect their fists.

H is for helmet.

Skiers wipe out on icy hills.
Football players tackle each other.
A baseball pitch can hit the batter.
Athletes wear helmets to protect
their heads.

I is for ice.

Ice is cold, hard, and slippery. Hockey players speed across the ice on their skates. Ice flies when a player stops.

J is for **jump ball**. As the basketball game begins, two players jump with their arms stretched high. Each player tries to get the ball for his team.

K is for **kick**.

A football kicker practices for the big game. He uses his kicking skills to punt. He also scores points for his team.

L is for lap.

Swimmers streak through the pool. They race to one end and back again. The best swimmers finish a lap in less than 30 seconds.

M is for **muscle**.

Athletes build strong muscles.
Gymnasts have arm muscles strong
enough to support their whole body.

N is for **net**.

In volleyball, it's all about getting the ball over the net. Set it, bump it, or spike it!

O is for **overtime**.

The score is tied, but time is up. The game goes into overtime. More time goes on the clock. Both teams try to score more points to win the game.

HOME   GUEST

TIME OUTS LEFT   DOWN   TO GO   BALL ON   QTR   TIME OUTS LEFT

P is for **puck**.

Hockey pucks are made of hard rubber. These 1-inch (2.5-centimeter) thick disks slide across the ice. Pucks are frozen before games to keep them from bouncing.

Q is for quarterback.

The quarterback is in charge on the football field. He looks for an open teammate. Then he sends the ball spiraling through the air. Touchdown!

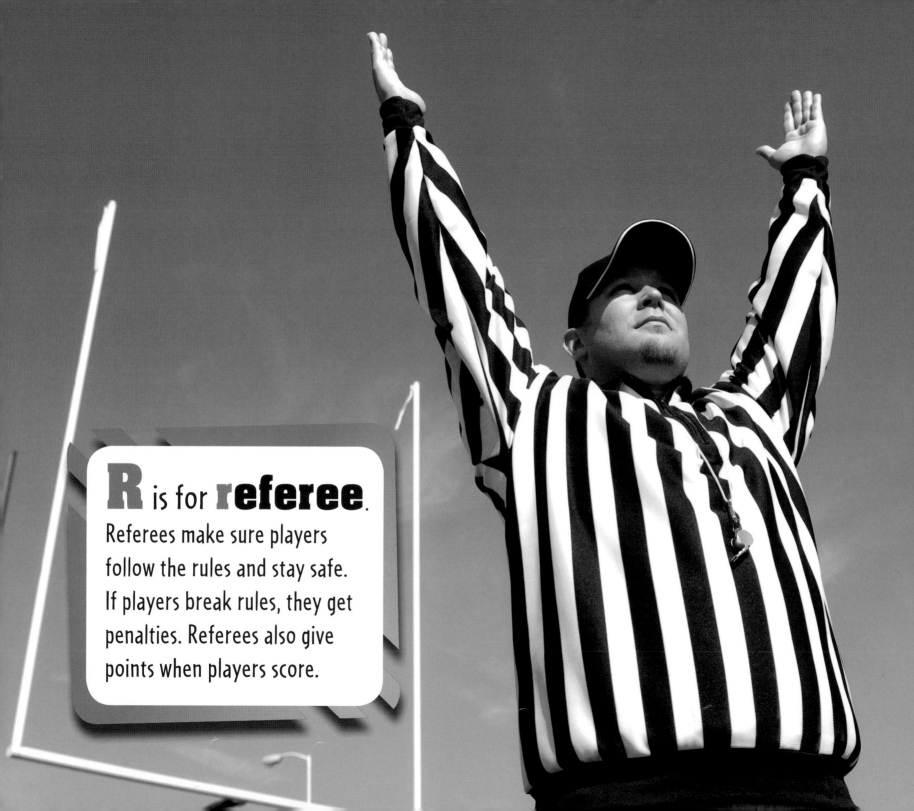

R is for referee.

Referees make sure players follow the rules and stay safe. If players break rules, they get penalties. Referees also give points when players score.

S is for score.

Soccer players score by kicking the ball into the goal. The team with more points wins the game.

T is for **tee**.

A golf ball sits on a tee. Players tee off when they hit the ball off of the tee. Professional golfers like Tiger Woods hit the ball about 900 feet (274 meters).

U is for uniform.

Players on a team wear matching uniforms. The home team usually wears white. The visiting team wears a dark color. Uniforms remind teammates to work together.

V is for **victory**.
In any sport, players want to win.
People cheer for you when you win.
And victory usually means a trophy!

W is for World Cup.

Every four years, soccer teams from around the world compete. The winning team keeps the solid gold trophy until the next World Cup.

X is for X Games.

The X Games started in 1995. X Gamers compete in extreme sports like skateboarding. Skateboarders speed up and down ramps. They fly high in the air during tricks.

Y is for yard line.

One yard is 3 feet (.9 meter) long. Football players run down the 100-yard (91-meter) field to score touchdowns.

Z is for **zone**.

A soccer goalie's zone is in front of the goal. In the zone, the goalie can touch the ball with his hands. He can also kick the ball.

Fun Facts about Sports

Most sports have a time limit. Baseball games have nine innings. Innings don't have a time limit. Professional baseball games last about three hours.

A golf ball has 300–500 dots called dimples. Dimples help the ball fly through the air.

Athletes from around the world compete in the Olympic Games. The first modern Olympic Games took place in Athens, Greece, in 1896.

Balls used in professional baseball games have exactly 108 stitches.

In 10th grade, basketball star Michael Jordan tried out for the varsity basketball team. But he was too short and skinny to play. A year later, he made the team and became a standout player.

It's hard to believe that Michael Phelps didn't like swimming as a kid. In 2008, he won eight gold medals at the Olympics. Phelps won one event by 1/100th of a second!

In 2004, baseball player Derek Jeter dove into the stands to catch a foul ball. He came up bleeding, but he made the catch.

Bicycle motocross (BMX) riding is an extreme sport. BMX bikers ride up one side of a U-shaped ramp. Then they fly into the air to do flips and spins. Dave Mirra was the first BMX rider to land a double backflip in a contest.

Glossary

athlete (ATH-leet) — a person trained in a sport or game

compete (kuhm-PEET) — to try hard to outdo others at a race or contest

dribble (DRI-buhl) — to bounce a basketball off the floor using one hand

extreme (ek-STREEM) — very dangerous or difficult

foul (FOUL) — an action that is against the rules

limit (LIM-it) — to keep within a certain amount; many sports have time limits.

penalty (PEN-uhl-tee) — a punishment for breaking the rules

professional (pruh-FESH-uh-nuhl) — a person who receives money for taking part in a sport or activity

punt (PUHNT) — a kick where the ball is dropped from the hands and kicked before it touches the ground

stadium (STAY-dee-uhm) — a large building in which sports events are held

stitch (STITCH) — a loop of yarn produced by sewing

tackle (TAK-uhl) — to stop another player by knocking him or her to the ground

Read More

Herzog, Brad. *A Is for Amazing Moments: A Sports Alphabet.* Chelsea, Mich.: Sleeping Bear Press, 2008.

Salzmann, Mary Elizabeth. *Angling to Zorbing: Sports from A to Z.* Let's See A to Z. Edina, Minn.: ABDO, 2008.

Zuehlke, Jeffrey. *Michael Phelps.* Amazing Athletes. Minneapolis: Lerner, 2009.

Internet Sites

FactHound offers a safe, fun way to find Internet sites related to this book. All of the sites on FactHound have been researched by our staff.

Here's all you do:

Visit *www.facthound.com*

FactHound will fetch the best sites for you!

Index

athletes, 2, 6, 9, 14, 28

baseball, 3, 7, 9, 28, 29
basketball, 3, 5, 11, 29
BMX, 29
boxing, 8

coaches, 4

dribbling, 5

football, 9, 12, 18, 26

golf, 21, 28
gymnasts, 14

helmets, 9
hockey, 10, 17

Jeter, Derek, 29
Jordan, Michael, 29

Mirra, Dave, 29

Olympic Games, 28

Phelps, Michael, 29
practice, 2, 4, 12

referees, 19, 27

skateboarding, 25
skiing, 9
soccer, 3, 20, 24, 27
stadiums, 6
swimming, 13, 29

uniforms, 22

victory, 23
volleyball, 15

Woods, Tiger, 21
World Cup, 24

X Games, 25

A+ Books are published by Capstone Press,
151 Good Counsel Drive, P.O. Box 669, Mankato, Minnesota 56002.
www.capstonepress.com

Copyright © 2010 by Capstone Press, a Capstone imprint.
All rights reserved.
No part of this publication may be reproduced in whole or in part, or stored in a retrieval system,
or transmitted in any form or by any means, electronic, mechanical, photocopying, recording,
or otherwise, without written permission of the publisher.
For information regarding permission, write to Capstone Press,
151 Good Counsel Drive, P.O. Box 669, Dept. R, Mankato, Minnesota 56002.
Printed in the United States of America in North Mankato, Minnesota.
092009
005618CGS10

 Books published by Capstone Press are manufactured with paper
containing at least 10 percent post-consumer waste.

Library of Congress Cataloging-in-Publication Data
Salas, Laura Purdie.
S is for score!: a sports alphabet / By Laura Purdie Salas.
   p. cm. — (A+ Books. Alphabet fun)
   Includes bibliographical references and index.
   Summary: "Introduces different sports through photographs and brief text that uses one word
relating to the subject for each letter of the alphabet" — Provided by publisher.
   ISBN 978-1-4296-3915-6 (library binding)
   ISBN 978-1-4296-4833-2 (paperback)
   1. Sports — Juvenile literature. 2. Alphabet — Juvenile literature. I. Title. II. Series.
GV705.4.S33 2010
796 — dc22 [E]   2009035195

Credits
Abby Czeskleba, editor; Matt Bruning, designer; Wanda Winch, media researcher;
   Laura Manthe, production specialist; Sarah Schuette, photo stylist; Marcy Morin, scheduler

Photo Credits
Capstone Studio/Karon Dubke, cover, back cover, 4, 7, 10, 12, 16, 17, 19, 21, 23, 26, 28; CORBIS/epa/
Michael Hanschke, 1, 20; Getty Images Inc./WireImage/Phillip Ellsworth, 25; Shutterstock: aceshot1,
6, Eoghan McNally, 24, Epic Stock, 13, Galina Barskaya, 14, Jack Dagley Photography, 8, Jerry
Sharp, 18, Jim Parkin, 22, JustASC, 3, Matthew Jacques, 11, Pete Niesen, 2, Rui Alexandre Araujo, 27,
Sportsphotographer.eu, 9, Valeria73, 15, vospalej, 5

Note to Parents, Teachers, and Librarians
Alphabet Fun books use bold art and photographs and topics with high appeal to engage young
children in learning. Compelling nonfiction content educates and entertains while propelling readers
toward mastery of the alphabet. These books are designed to be read aloud to a pre-reader or read
independently by an early reader. The images help children understand the text and concepts discussed.
Alphabet Fun books support further learning by including the following sections: Fun Facts, Glossary,
Read More, Internet Sites, and Index. Early readers may need assistance using these features.